For the intangible world

When I was a child, I liked to listen to my grandma talk about the past. She talked a lot about my grandpa, who died before I was born. His death affected everyone in the family. When I was young, I had no idea how difficult life was but could see that my grandpa's death inspired my family to work harder and become more intimate with one another. I saw that my grandpa's life still existed in every family member who loved him. My love for my family made this book happen.

Because I never met my grandpa, my imagination has become unlimited. I imagined Grandpa integrating with the universe, which is rich, abstract, and detailed. Sometimes I can feel the intangible world when I see the world with my heart.

—Jin

ABOUT THIS BOOK

The illustrations for this book were done in colored pencil, watercolor, marker, oil pastel, acrylic, dip pen, pencil, ink, and brush on watercolor paper and drawing paper. This book was edited by Alvina Ling and Nikki Garcia and designed by Dave Caplan and Kelly Brennan. The production was supervised by Erika Schwartz, and the production editor was Marisa Finkelstein. The text was set in Sassoon Infant, and the display type is hand-lettered.

Copyright © 2019 by Jin Xiaojing · Cover illustration copyright © 2019 by Jin Xiaojing. Cover design by Dave Caplan. · Cover copyright © 2019 by Hachette Book Group, Inc. · Hachette Book Group supports the right to free expression and the value of copyright. The purpose of copyright is to encourage writers and artists to produce the creative works that enrich our culture. The scanning, uploading, and distribution of this book without permission is a theft of the author's intellectual property. If you would like permission to use material from the book (other than for review purposes), please contact permissions@hbgusa.com. Thank you for your support of the author's rights. · Little, Brown and Company · Hachette Book Group · 1290 Avenue of the Americas, New York, NY 10104 · Visit us at LBYR.com · First Edition: September 2019 · Little, Brown and Company is a division of Hachette Book Group, Inc. · The Little, Brown name and logo are trademarks of Hachette Book Group, Inc. · The publisher is not responsible for websites (or their content) that are not owned by the publisher. · Library of Congress Cataloging-in-Publication Data · Names: Xiaojing, Jin, author, illustrator. · Title: I miss my grandpa / Jin Xiaojing. · Description: First edition. I New York ; Boston : Little, Brown and Company, 2019. I Summary: A child asks different family members about her late grandfather and learns of his characteristics through the features he passed down to his children and grandchildren. · Identifiers: LCCN 2018050085I ISBN 9780316417877 (hardcover) I ISBN 9780316417860 (ebook) I ISBN 9780316417891 (library edition ebook) · Subjects: I CYAC: Grandfathers—Fiction. I Heredity—Fiction. I Family life—Fiction. · Classification: LCC PZ7.1.X56 Iam 2019 I DDC [E]—dc23 · LC record available at https://lccn.loc.gov/2018050085 · ISBNs: 978-0-316-41787-7 (hardcover), 978-0-316-41786-0 (ebook), 978-0-316-41790-7 (ebook), 978-0-316-41791-4 (ebook) · PRINTED IN CHINA · APS · 10 9 8 7 6 5 4 3 2 1

I MISS MY GRANDPA

EVEN THOUGH
~~I'VE NEVER MET HIM~~

JIN XIAOJING

L **B**
LITTLE, BROWN AND COMPANY
New York · Boston

I've never met my grandpa. He died before I was born, but still I have always felt like he's here with me.

I want to know everything about him. So I like to ask my grandma,

"What did Grandpa look like?"

Grandma answers,
"Your youngest uncle, Mason,
has a face
shaped most like your grandpa's."

Uncle Mason says,
"Your grandpa's face is very
far away, like the moon, in my memory.
Although sometimes I still dream about him."

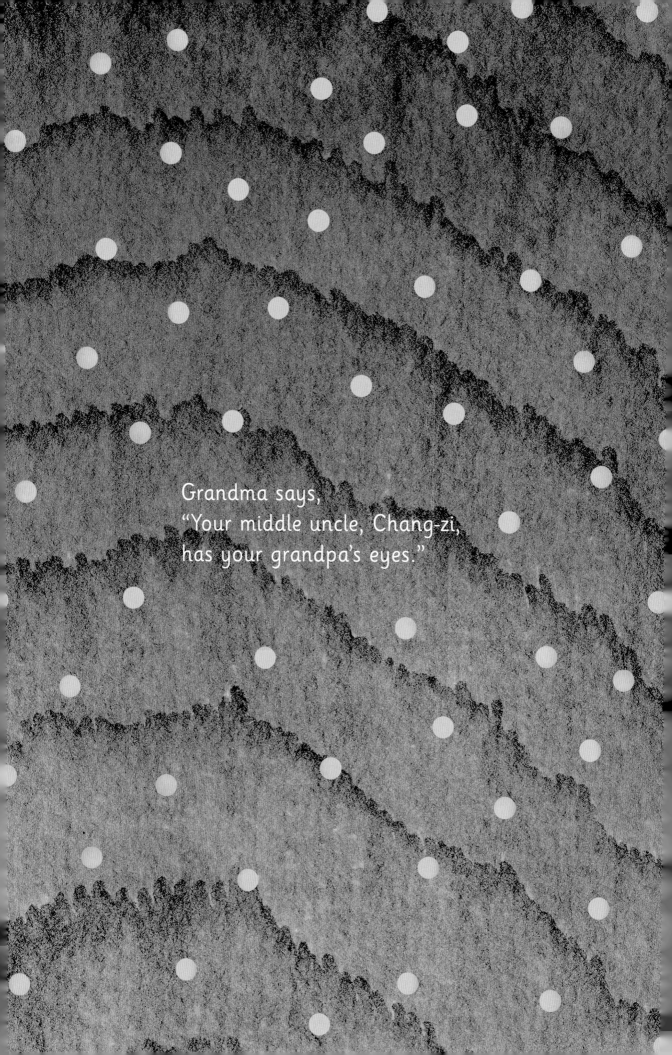

Grandma says,
"Your middle uncle, Chang-zi,
has your grandpa's eyes."

Uncle Chang-zi says,
"When your grandpa looked at the world,
he was quiet and patient like a crocodile.
When he closed his eyes, his imagination sparked."

Grandma says,
"Your eldest uncle, Leo,
has a nose
passed down from your grandpa."

Uncle Leo says,
"By always learning,
trying, and practicing,
your grandpa knew
when to water the soil,
when to fertilize the soil,
and when to plant in the soil
just by smelling the soil."

My grandma says,
"Your aunt Zai-zi
has a mouth
most like your grandpa's."

My aunt Zai-zi says,

"Your grandpa told us stories night to night.

In his stories, he had a dove's voice,

duck's voice, lion's voice, lamb's voice,

cloud's voice, wind's voice,
sunrise's voice, sunset's voice,

and countless other voices."

Grandma says,
"Your eldest cousin, Aiden,
has ears like your grandpa.
When he listens, he doesn't talk.
He can hear the silence lying between
and underneath many sounds."

My cousin Aiden says nothing.
He just listens.

Grandma says,
"Your mom inherited
your grandpa's hair."

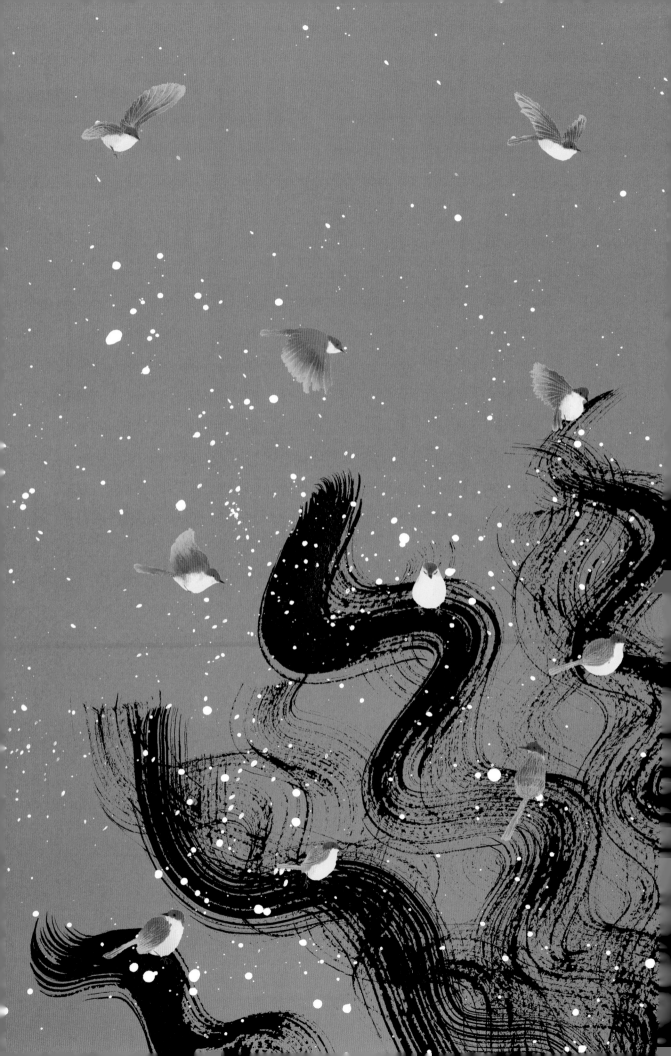

My mom says,
"Your grandpa's hair was
really curly like a nest—
birds even came to
stay in it one winter."

Does Grandpa look like this?

Does he look like this?

I miss my grandpa, even though I've never met him.
Grandma says, "You can meet him in your heart.
He is still living within us, who love him."

Grandma says, "You also have your grandpa's hair."

MANDARIN CHINESE TRANSLATION

I've never met my grandpa.
He died before I was born,
but still I have always felt like he's here with me.
I want to know everything about him.
So I like to ask my grandma,
"What did Grandpa look like?"

我从来没有见过外公。他在我出生前就去世了，
但我常常感到他一直陪伴在我们身边。我想知道
关于他的一切。所以我问外婆，"外公是什么样
子呀？"
Wǒ cóng lái méi yǒu jiàn guò wài gōng。Tā zài wǒ
chū shēng qián jiù qù shì le，dàn wǒ cháng cháng
gǎn dào tā yī zhí péi bàn zài wǒ men shēn biān。Wǒ
xiǎng zhī dào guān yú tā de yī qiè。Suǒ yǐ wǒ wèn
Wàipó，"Wàigōng shì shén me yàng zǐ ya？"

Grandma answers,
"Your youngest uncle, Mason,
has a face
shaped most like your grandpa's."

Uncle Mason says,
"Your grandpa's face is very
far away, like the moon, in my memory.
Although sometimes I still dream about him."

外婆说，"你马森舅舅的脸型像你外公。"
马森舅舅说，"你外公的模样在记忆里已经很模
糊了，就像那月亮。虽然有时候我还是会梦到
他。"
Wàipó shuō，"Nǐ Mǎsēn jiù jiù de liǎn xíng xiàng nǐ wài
gōng。"
Mǎsēn jiù jiù shuō，"Nǐ wài gōng de mó yàng zài jì yì
lǐ yǐ jīng hěn mó hú le，jiù xiàng nà yuè liàng。Suī rán
yǒu shí hòu wǒ hái shì huì mèng dào tā。"

Grandma says,
"Your middle uncle, Chang-zi,
has your grandpa's eyes."

Uncle Chang-zi says,
"When your grandpa looked at the world,
he was quiet and patient like a crocodile.
When he closed his eyes, his imagination
sparked."

外婆说，"你场子舅舅有你外公的眼睛。"
场子舅舅说，"当你外公观察着世界的时候，他
安静和耐心的像一只鳄鱼。每当他闭上眼睛，他
的想象就会开始闪现。"
Wàipó shuō，"Nǐ Chǎngzǐ jiù jiù yǒu nǐ wài gōng de
yǎn jīng。"
Chǎngzǐ jiù jiù shuō，"Dāng nǐ wài gōng guān chá zhe
shì jiè de shí hòu，tā ān jìng hé nài xīn de xiàng yī zhī
è yú。Měi dāng tā bì shàng yǎn jīng，tā de xiǎng xiàng
jiù huì kāi shǐ shǎn xiàn。"

Grandma says,
"Your eldest uncle, Leo,
has a nose
passed down from your grandpa."

Uncle Leo says,
"By always learning,
trying, and practicing,
your grandpa knew
when to water the soil,
when to fertilize the soil,
and when to plant in the soil
just by smelling the soil."

外婆说，"你大舅里偶的鼻子遗传自你外公。"
里偶舅舅说，"通过不断的学习，尝试和练习，你
外公闻一闻土就知道何时浇水，何时施肥，又何
时播种。"
Wàipó shuō，"Nǐ dà jiù Lǐǒu de bí zǐ yí chuán zì nǐ wài
gōng。"
Lǐǒu jiù jiù shuō，"Tōng guò bú duàn de xué xí，cháng
shì hé liàn xí，nǐ wài gōng wén yī wén tǔ jiù zhī dào hé
shí jiāo shuǐ，hé shí shī féi，yòu hé shí bō zhǒng。"